Emily and Alice Again

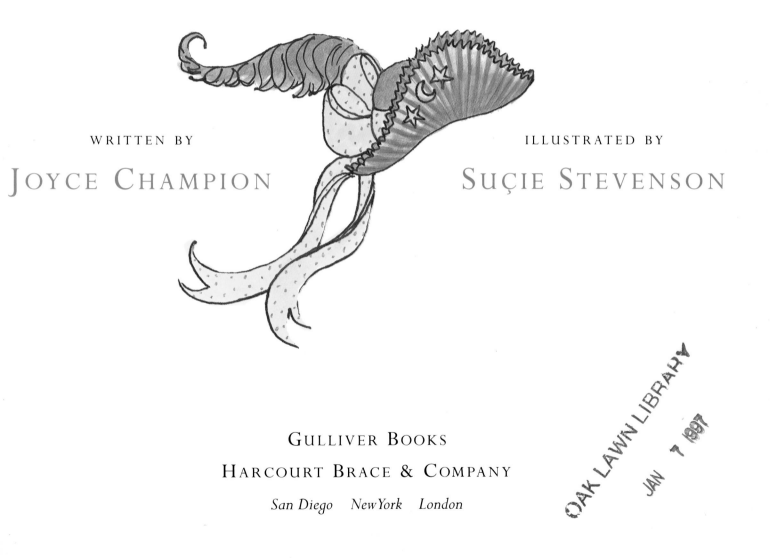

WRITTEN BY

JOYCE CHAMPION

ILLUSTRATED BY

SUÇIE STEVENSON

GULLIVER BOOKS

HARCOURT BRACE & COMPANY

San Diego   New York   London

Gulliver Books is a registered trademark of Harcourt Brace & Company.

Library of Congress Cataloging-in-Publication Data
Champion, Joyce.
Emily and Alice again/Joyce Champion; illustrated by Suçie Stevenson.
p.   cm.
"Gulliver books."
Summary: Two best friends trade sunglasses for a sister,
wear new hats, and have a sleepover.
ISBN 0-15-200439-4
[1. Friendship — Fiction]   I. Stevenson, Suçie, ill.   II. Title.
PZ7.C3585En   1995
[E] — dc20   93-5004

Printed in Singapore
First edition
A B C D E

The illustrations in this book were done in
acrylic and indelible felt-tip pen on Bristol Vellum.
The display type was set in Egmont by Photo-Lettering, New York, New York.
The text type was set in Perpetua by Thompson Type, San Diego, California.
Color separations were made by Bright Arts, Ltd., Singapore.
Printed and bound by Tien Wah Press, Singapore
This book was printed with soya-based inks on Leykam recycled paper,
which contains more than 20 percent postconsumer waste and has a total
recycled content of at least 50 percent.
Production supervision by Warren Wallerstein and Diana Ford
Designed by Trina Stahl and Lori J. McThomas

For Dave

— J. C.

To my dear, dear sister Jane

— S. S.

The Trade

Emily ran over to her best friend Alice's house. "*Oooh,* Alice, where did you get those cool sunglasses?" she asked.

"My grandma sent them to me from Florida," said Alice. "Here, you can try them on."

Emily tried on Alice's new sunglasses. She looked up at the sky. She looked down at the ground. Everything looked pink and happy.

"I *love* these sunglasses," said Emily. "I could wear them forever." At that moment she knew she had to have them.

Alice watched Emily suspiciously. "I want my sunglasses back now," she said.

Emily gave Alice her sunglasses. But she had a plan. "Don't move," she told Alice. "I'll be right back."

Emily ran to her house. She came back to Alice's holding two stuffed animals. "Want to trade Zippidy and Doodah for your new sunglasses?" she asked.

"Don't you have your own sunglasses?" asked Alice.

"I only have the plain round kind," answered Emily. "I don't have cool heart-shaped glasses like yours. I don't have sunglasses that make the world pink and happy. Let's trade."

Alice looked at Emily's bears and shook her head. "Sorry, Emily," she said. "No trade."

"I'll be right back," said Emily.

Emily returned to Alice's holding a box. "I'll trade you my favorite rocks," she said, "even all the sparkly ones, if I can have your sunglasses."

Alice looked at Emily's rock collection and shook her head. "Sorry, Emily," she said. "Still no trade."

"OK," said Emily, "wait here — because I'll be back."

Emily ran to her house again. She *had* to find something to trade. She walked in circles around her room. Then she saw her little sister, Nora, in the doorway. This was her best idea yet!

Emily grabbed her sister's hand and ran back to Alice's.

"Alice," she said, "I'll trade my favorite sister — my *only* sister — for your new sunglasses."

Alice looked at Nora. She looked at her chubby little legs and tiny red sneakers. Alice nodded. "OK, I'll trade!"

Alice gave Emily her new sunglasses. Emily gave Alice her only sister.

Emily ran home and put on her new sunglasses. Everything looked pink and happy. "I am a beautiful movie star," she said to the mirror. Then she ran out back.

Emily lay on a beach chair. She looked up at the pink sun. She watched pink clouds float by. "I am on a big cruise ship," she said to the sky. "Soon I will be on a faraway island."

Emily heard giggles coming from Alice's backyard. She could see that Alice was teaching Nora how to do cartwheels. *I'm glad they're having fun,* she thought.

Emily polished her sunglasses. She looked over at Alice's yard again. She watched Alice put on a puppet show for Nora. She watched Alice give Nora horseback rides. She heard Nora laugh and shriek. *They're REALLY having fun,* thought Emily.

Emily put her sunglasses on. She looked up at the sky. She looked down at the ground. The world was still pink. But it didn't seem quite so happy.

Emily yanked off the glasses and ran next door. "Alice," she said, "I think I've had enough fun with your cool sunglasses."

Alice tried to catch her breath. "I think I've had enough fun with your sister," she said.

Emily gave back Alice's sunglasses. Alice waved good-bye to Nora.

"Let's just *borrow* next time, OK?" asked Alice.

"Good idea," said Emily.

Alice smiled and put on her sunglasses.

Emily smiled as she and Nora cartwheeled home.

The New Hat

Emily was waiting on Alice's front step. "Hurry up, Alice!" she called. "It's time for school."

Alice peeked out. Slowly she opened the door. "OK, Emily, I'm coming out. But don't laugh at my new hat," she said.

Emily walked all around Alice, looking at her new hat. She touched the velvet ribbon. She stroked the long, blue feather. "I've never seen a hat like this before, Alice," she said.

"I picked it out myself. Do you think it's silly or goofy-looking?" asked Alice.

"No," said Emily. "I think it's wonderful."

Alice smiled at Emily. "I think so, too," she said. "I'm going to wear it to school."

Emily and Alice picked up their backpacks. As they walked to school, Alice's blue feather bounced up and down.

When they turned the corner, they saw Chuckie Jones. Chuckie pointed and laughed. "Is that a hat?" he called. "Or is a peacock sitting on your head?"

Alice's face turned red. "Oh, Emily," she said. "This *is* a silly hat. It looks like a peacock."

"Don't listen to Chuckie Jones," said Emily. "What does he know about hats anyway?"

Emily and Alice walked on. They passed the Tupper twins, Randy and Robin.

The twins flapped their arms and giggled. "Look at Alice's hat!" called Robin.

"It's getting ready to fly away," said Randy.

Alice hid behind Emily. "See? This *is* a goofy-looking hat," said Alice. "It looks like it will fly away."

"Don't listen to Randy or Robin," said Emily. "They don't know anything about hats either."

Emily and Alice walked past Burton the bulldog. Burton jumped up and howled at Alice's hat.

"Even Burton doesn't like my hat!" cried Alice. "It's silly *and* goofy-looking, and I'll never wear it again!"

Alice yanked off her hat and stuffed it into her backpack. She walked the rest of the way to school feeling sad.

That afternoon Emily hurried home. She ran to her room
and grabbed her coin bank. "Can we please go downtown?"
she asked her mother. "I need to get something."

The next morning Emily sat waiting on Alice's front step. She was wearing a new hat.

"Emily!" exclaimed Alice when she opened the door. "You have a hat just like mine!" Alice walked all around Emily, inspecting her new hat. She touched the velvet ribbon. She stroked the long, blue feather.

"How do I look?" asked Emily.

"Well," said Alice, "the *hat* is silly and goofy-looking, but somehow *you* look wonderful!"

That morning Emily and Alice both wore their new hats. Chuckie Jones pointed and laughed. Randy and Robin flapped and giggled. Burton the bulldog howled.

But Emily and Alice held their heads high. And the two friends with their two blue feathers bounced all the way to school.

The Scary Sleepover

One Friday Emily invited Alice to sleep over. Alice had never slept at a friend's house, but she was excited about her first sleepover at Emily's.

Before bedtime Emily and Alice did gymnastics on Emily's bed. They polished each other's toenails and told every knock-knock joke they knew.

After they'd finished their peanut butter cookies and milk, Emily's mother hugged the girls and turned out the light.

Emily's room was dark and quiet. It was *too* dark and quiet. Alice lay wide awake.

"Emily! Emily!" called Alice suddenly. "Something's wrong!"

Emily yawned. "What's the matter, Alice?" she asked.

"Your room is much too *dark,*" said Alice. "The Snapigator could be in here."

"The Snapigator?" asked Emily. "What's the Snapigator?"

"The Snapigator lives under beds," replied Alice. "He crawls out on dark nights."

"Oh, Alice," said Emily. "Don't be silly. The Snapigator doesn't live here."

Emily and Alice each rolled over. Emily was just about to fall asleep when Alice shouted, "Emily! Emily!"

"*Now* what is it?" asked Emily.

"Your room is much too *quiet,*" said Alice. "When it's this quiet, you can hear the Secret Sisters."

"The Secret Sisters?" said Emily. "Who are they?"

Alice sat straight up. "The Secret Sisters hide in quiet bedroom closets. They tell terrible secrets all night long."

Emily giggled. "Oh, Alice," she said. "Don't be silly. The Secret Sisters don't live here."

"Are you sure?" asked Alice.

Emily got out of bed and opened her closet door. "Listen," she said. "I don't hear any Secret Sisters. Do you?"

Alice shook her head and sighed with relief. She began to feel sleepy. "I'm sure you're right, Emily," she said. "The Snapigator and the Secret Sisters don't live here."

Alice curled up in her sleeping bag and closed her eyes. Now Emily lay wide awake.

Emily listened carefully to the quiet in her room. She peeked into the darkness under her bed. Then she jumped up and shook Alice.

"Alice! Alice! Wake up!" she shouted. "I just thought of something! Maybe the Snapigator and Secret Sisters don't *live* here, but they could still come and visit."

Emily and Alice looked at each other.

Emily switched on the light. Alice turned on the radio and jumped into Emily's bed. They pulled up the covers . . . and fell asleep holding hands.